GRASHKOR
THE BEAST GUARD

With special thanks to Michael Ford
To Callum Leslie

www.beastquest.co.uk

ORCHARD BOOKS
Carmelite House
50 Victoria Embankment
London EC4Y 0DZ

A Paperback Original
First published in Great Britain in 2012

Beast Quest is a registered trademark of Beast Quest Limited
Series created by Beast Quest Limited, London

Text © Beast Quest Limited 2012
Cover by Steve Sims © Beast Quest Limited 2012
Inside illustrations by Dynamo © Beast Quest Limited 2012

A CIP catalogue record for this book is available
from the British Library.

ISBN 978 1 40831 517 0

5 7 9 10 8 6

Printed and bound by CPI Group (UK) Ltd, Croydon, CR0 4YY

The paper and board used in this book are made from wood from
responsible sources.

Orchard Books is an imprint of Hachette Children's Group
and published by The Watts Publishing Group Limited,
an Hachette UK company.

www.hachette.co.uk

GRASHKOR
THE BEAST GUARD

BY ADAM BLADE

ORCHARD

WESTERN OCEAN

THE FOREST OF FEAR

THE RUBY DESERT

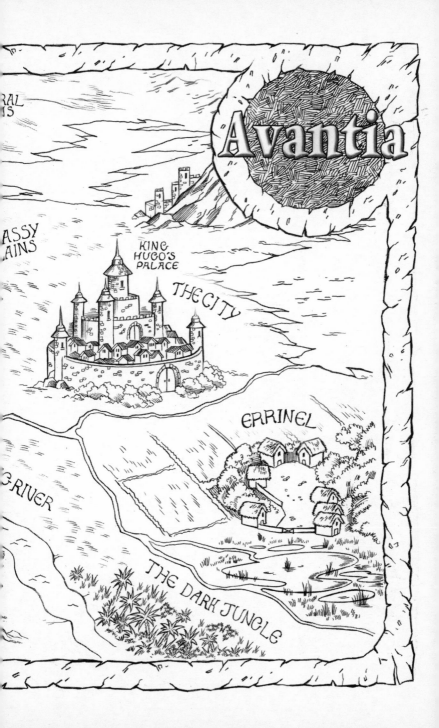

STORY ONE

Where am I? Silver, where are you?

My head hurts and my mouth is dry. When I rub my eyes clear, I can see...nothing. Just darkness and gloom. I can feel a dank, dirty stone floor beneath me, and damp stone walls around me.

I'm in some kind of cell!

I'm starting to remember what happened... I remember my journey, down the long road. The highwaymen... Then my mind goes blank, and I remember nothing else. But I know who's responsible – that Evil Wizard!

I don't know how long I can last here or what dangers lie beyond the locked door. Does Tom even know I'm here? He's my only hope now.

Death may await me, but I won't cower before it. I will stay strong.

Elenna

CHAPTER ONE

LURKING DANGER

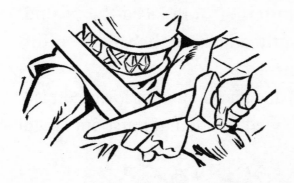

The two youths drew their swords and edged towards Tom. The one on the left was taller. He bore a scar on his chin, and sweat dripped from his brow.

His companion, a squat young man, grinned. "We've got him now, Harris," he said.

As the youth lunged, Tom deflected the blow with a low block of his

sword, and darted around him.
The attacker plunged head-first into
a horse trough, carried by his
momentum. He came up again,
spluttering. Tom faced the second
youth, adjusting the shield on his
arm.

The taller opponent lowered his
wooden sword and burst out laughing.

"I think the boy's got you, Roger!" he said, pointing to his sodden companion.

Tom smiled too. Roger did look funny, with his hair dripping wet and his mouth agape. "I think maybe that's enough practice for today," Tom said. "Roger, you need to work on your balance and footwork. Harris, make sure you keep your shield tight to your body. A blade could slip through."

Both cadets nodded and walked away. Tom rested his wooden practice sword in the equipment rack and retrieved his belt and scabbard.

Across the Palace courtyard, Captain Harkman was taking another group of trainee soldiers through an advance-and-retreat drill.

They're already getting good, Tom

thought, as the young men huddled close, protecting each other's flanks with their shields. It had only been a few days since the fresh batch of cadets had gathered. Recruitment orders had gone out, and boys had come from all over the villages of the kingdom, proud to enlist in King Hugo's army. The training was hard work, but for the moment they were having fun. Soon the training with real weapons would begin.

I just hope they never have to put their skills into practice, Tom thought.

But Tom knew the future was uncertain.

A month ago, King Hugo had led his most experienced soldiers out to the eastern frontier. Beyond the Forbidden Land, they'd faced a Barbarian invasion. Tom had offered to go too, but the King had shaken his head.

"I need you to stay and train the army reserves," he'd said, "just in case the Barbarians break through."

Tom had nodded, disappointed but also ready to do his duty. There was no shortage of other threats in Avantia. Tom cast a glance towards a section of the outer wall that was being repaired. Somehow the young witch Petra had cast a spell to blast her way out of the Palace dungeon. She'd been held there since they'd returned from their last Quest in the Kingdom of Seraph. With Petra on the loose, the kingdom was not safe. Guided by her twisted magic, Evil Beasts might strike at any moment.

Tom saw a boy rushing across the yard carrying several quivers full of

arrows over his shoulder. A group of
archers waited beside a straw-stuffed
sack-figure target and one girl was
bending her bow with strong arms.

"Keep practising," Tom called, "and
you'll be a match for Elenna one
day!"

The girl archer smiled at him.
*Elenna would be able to put an arrow
through the figure's eye from fifty paces*,
Tom thought.

He missed his friend. She'd wanted
to fight in the east too, but King
Hugo had ordered that she remain in
Avantia in case danger struck. She'd
set out for her Uncle Leo's house in
the southwest two days ago. *She'll
almost be there by now*, Tom thought.

He headed towards the Palace to
visit Aduro. The Good Wizard was
monitoring events at the frontier

with his magic ball. Tom heard the patter of feet behind him. He turned to find a red-cheeked boy clutching two wooden swords.

"What can I do for you, Sebastian?" Tom asked.

"I've been practising my block and roll," the boy replied.

Tom grinned. Sebastian was his star pupil, much better at duelling than most boys twice his size.

"Show me, then," said Tom, reaching out and taking the other sword.

Sebastian stood at guard, his sword outstretched. Tom stabbed. With a deft side-step, the boy knocked Tom's sword aside, and turned right around on his heel. His sword-arm flicked round too, and Tom ducked beneath the blow. "Excellent!" Tom said.

Sebastian lunged and Tom had to be quick to step and block. Their blades rattled together. He pushed the boy's blade down and tried to swipe over the top, but Sebastian leant back and the blade swished harmlessly where his chest had been. Tom took advantage and stepped forwards while Sebastian was off-balance. With the lightest of pushes, Sebastian fell on his backside.

"You sacrificed your balance to avoid the blow," Tom said. "Always move your feet rather than your body when you dodge."

Sebastian arched his back, flicked up his legs and leapt to his feet without using his hands. He advanced on Tom with a series of quick slashes, driving Tom back.

He's quick! Tom thought, defending

the blows and looking for an
opening. From the corner of his eye,
he noticed that Captain Harkman's
recruits had stopped training to
watch. So had the archers and
some horse-riders.

"The boy's good!" called Roger.

Tom managed to stop Sebastian's
advance with a low jab that whistled
past the boy's knee. They circled each

other, both breathing heavily.

"You're getting better," Tom said. "Ready to carry on?"

Sebastian nodded, and Tom tossed his sword into his left hand, confusing his opponent. He gave two diagonal swipes, forcing Sebastian to retreat. The crowd parted to make way. Tom swapped hands again, feinting twice to the left. Sebastian dropped his guard awkwardly.

Squelch!

Sebastian's right foot slid out from underneath him and he fell to the ground – he'd slipped in a pile of horse manure. Tom placed his wooden blade softly against the boy's neck.

The crowd cheered and clapped as Sebastian looked in dismay at his foot.

"*Urgh!*" he said. "You only beat me because I slipped!"

"Always be aware of your surroundings," Tom said, offering a hand to help Sebastian up. The boy took it with a grin.

Tom remembered when he'd played at being a soldier, back at his Uncle Henry's house. He'd spent every evening with his wooden sword, pretending to fight enemies of the kingdom. That seemed like another lifetime.

"I'll keep training," said Sebastian.

"If you do, you'll be a great warrior one day," said Tom.

As Sebastian dusted himself off, his brow creased into a frown and his eyes flicked to something behind Tom.

Tom turned to see a grey dog

hobbling through the castle entrance.

No – not a dog!

"Silver!" Tom gasped.

"It's Elenna's wolf!" someone in the crowd muttered.

When Silver's eyes fell on Tom, he let out a weak howl and scampered over. Tom crouched to meet him, and as the wolf approached, Tom saw a black mark scorched across his side, a patch of hair burnt away. Silver

whined as Tom's fingers traced the wound. "It's all right, boy," he said.

Fear spread through Tom's chest, mirrored in the anxious eyes of those who crowded round. Silver's injuries weren't serious.

But where is Elenna? Tom thought.

CHAPTER TWO

WINDOW TO THE PAST

The Good Wizard Aduro squatted beside Silver, examining him. "He seems to be in good health," he said. "The question is, who did this to him?"

"Only one person would attack unprovoked," said Tom. He met Aduro's eyes.

"Malvel," muttered the Wizard.

"I thought he was forbidden to

enter the kingdom," said Tom.

"His magic is powerful and far-reaching," replied Aduro. "Even from other kingdoms. And if he's attacked Silver, he's probably attacked…"

"Elenna! But she's still on the journey to her uncle's!" Tom said. "We have no way of knowing where on the southwest road she encountered him." He pointed to Aduro's crystal ball, cradled in its stand on its podium and covered with a brown cloth. "Could you use that to find her?"

Aduro stroked Silver's ears and shook his head. "Someone – and I suspect Malvel's minion Petra – has meddled with the ball's magic. Its power is not what it once was."

Tom punched a fist into the palm of his hand. Silver growled at the sudden noise.

"We must remain calm, Tom," said the Wizard.

"How can I?" Tom asked. "Silver would never abandon Elenna unless something was seriously wrong. If Malvel's taken her, we don't know how long she's got left!" Panic gripped his heart. "She might even be…"

Aduro took him by the shoulders.

"Don't say that!" he said. "Don't ever speak those words!"

Tom felt a blush of shame redden his cheeks. "I'm sorry," he said.

Aduro let go. "All is not lost. There might be something we can do."

As Tom watched, the Wizard laid his open palm over the top of Silver's head. The wolf's ears twitched and a blue glow swelled from Aduro's

wrinkled hand. Light snaked in
smoky tendrils, enveloping Silver's
head. Then, without a sound, the
wolf's eyes rolled back in their
sockets and he flopped to the ground.

"What have you done to him?"
asked Tom in astonishment.

"Don't fear for your loyal
companion," said Aduro, walking
across to a small cupboard. "Silver
hasn't been harmed. The blue light

was a simple sleep charm – even a new apprentice can master that spell."

"Why does he need to be asleep?" asked Tom.

Aduro's eyes narrowed: "So I can look into his mind!"

The Wizard threw open the cupboard door and rooted around inside. Tom blinked, thinking his eyes were playing tricks on him. The inside of the cupboard looked three times the size of the door. Shelves lined each side, and Tom saw metal tripods, jars of strange liquid, and dusty tomes. *It must be a magical cupboard!* he thought.

Aduro reached deep inside until his head and shoulders had disappeared way past where the wall should have been. "Ah, here it is!" he said.

He drew out a strange object: a thin

piece of wood – willow, Tom guessed – which had been twisted into a circle and knotted together at the base with twine. In the hoop that it formed was a web of fine silver thread. Long, tawny eagle feathers had been tied to one side of the hoop, and from the other dangled a row of red and black beads.

"What is that thing?" Tom asked.

Aduro held the object up to the light, making it glitter. "This is a dream-catcher!" he said. "I've never used it on an animal before, but it might just work."

He knelt beside Silver and held the dream-catcher over the wolf's sleeping head. The Wizard closed his eyes and muttered an incantation under his breath.

Almost at once, the feathers

hanging from the dream-catcher ruffled and the beads swayed as if caught in a breeze – but Tom felt no wind on his skin. The fine hairs on Silver's head seemed to lift a fraction and from them seeped another puff of blue smoke. The faint cloud rose to meet the dream-catcher's strands and on the other side grew into a swollen sphere shape.

In the midst of the bubble, Tom made out an image forming – a brown swathe travelling through green.

"A road!" he said. "Is this Silver's dream?"

"It's a memory," said Aduro.

The image became clearer. They were seeing things through Silver's eyes. A figure appeared to one side, walking slightly ahead. Elenna! She was carrying her bow across one

shoulder and a bag of provisions over
the other. Her mouth opened and
a distant, washed-out voice drifted
through the chamber where Tom
was watching.

"Come on, Silver," she said. "Not
far to go now."

"She must have almost reached
her Uncle's," said Tom.

Angry shouts sounded from the road ahead. "Hey, get off!"

Tom saw three men on the tree-shaded path ahead. One lay in a ditch – a merchant from the look of his fine clothing – while two bandits in dirty torn tunics tried to wrestle something from his grasp.

"Give us the purse, old man!" shouted one of the robbers.

Elenna dropped her bag and rushed forwards past Silver, whose growls filled the chamber. She nocked an arrow into her bow. "Leave him alone!"

The bandits looked up. "It's only a girl," one hissed. "She's more likely to hit herself than one of us!"

Elenna loosed an arrow, taking the cap off his head and pinning it to a tree trunk. The thief went pale. Elenna took out a second arrow and aimed, stepping closer. "That's the last chance I'll give you," she said.

Good work, Elenna! Tom thought.

Silver padded up to her, but as he came within a few paces of the men, he yapped oddly.

"What is it?" asked Elenna.

As soon as the words left her mouth, all three men blurred and vanished. *It's a trick!* thought Tom.

A flash of purple light filled Silver's vision and Tom saw Elenna blasted sideways as a bolt of energy struck her in the chest.

"No!" he shouted.

In the dream-vision, Silver spied a plump figure stepping from behind a tree, her fingertips glowing purple.

"Petra!" said Tom.

The image rushed towards the witch. *Silver's running at her*, Tom realised. But

Petra jerked her hand, and the image
jolted sideways, fading to indigo.

"Petra blasted him with magic,"
Tom said.

The vision dimmed, but Tom made
out Petra leaning over Elenna's body.
She was winding a rope around his
friend's wrists and ankles, fastening
the knots tight and giggling to herself.

The image faded to black.

CHAPTER THREE

FATE WORSE THAN DEATH

"It wasn't Malvel," said Tom. "It was Petra!"

"Wrong!" boomed Malvel's voice, making Tom jump. "Who do you think gives Petra her orders?"

Tom spun around, drawing his sword, but the room was empty apart from himself, Aduro and Silver.

"Show yourself, Malvel!" Aduro shouted.

"With pleasure!" sneered the
Evil Wizard.

Across the room, the brown satin
cloth fell away from the crystal ball.
In its shining surface appeared
Malvel's twisted features. Tom and
Aduro rushed to peer into it.

"Don't you dare hurt her!"
said Tom.

"Like you hurt me, you mean?"
said Malvel, his face darkening.
"Like when you pushed me into
that wretched Flame, banishing
me to Gorgonia?"

"You deserve your punishment,
and you'll never see Avantia again,"
said Tom.

"How fitting," said Malvel, his voice
an icy hiss. "Because you will never
see Elenna again either!"

Aduro gripped the ball, and

brought his face close to its surface.
"What have you done with her?"
he demanded.

"I thought you'd never ask,"
said Malvel. "Take a look."

The Evil Wizard's face faded,
replaced by swirling storm clouds.
Tom recognised the coastline of the
Western Ocean, at the furthest
reaches of the kingdom. The vision

left the sands, and travelled across
the rolling sea, with white-tipped
waves as black as lead. The ball
took them on a journey out into
the ocean.

Through the sheets of wind-swept
rain, a dark shape loomed. Tom saw
the battlements and towers of a
windowless castle, clinging to a spur

of rock. It was a place he'd never even known existed.

The image faded. Tom marched towards the door, his blood burning. He heard a click of fingers and the door slammed closed. Tom spun around to face Aduro. The wizard's face was ashen.

"Why did you do that? If Elenna's in that place, I have to go after her," he said.

"If Malvel has taken Elenna to the Chamber of Pain, she isn't going anywhere for a long time," replied Aduro. "There's nothing you can do."

Tom swallowed thickly. "The Chamber of Pain?"

Aduro replaced the cloth over the crystal ball, his hand trembling. "The Chamber is the most feared prison in all the Kingdoms. Few even know of its existence. The dungeon houses only the most dangerous criminals and wicked minds – those who should never be released."

Tom yanked on the door handle, but it remained closed. "Well, I'm not going to leave Elenna to rot there," he said. "Let me out!"

"Wait a moment," said Aduro. "I won't stop you from going to the island, but I will warn you first. The Chamber of Pain can be reached only by magic – the sea, as you saw, is treacherous beyond measure."

"I've faced high seas before," said Tom. "It won't stop me."

"But even if you defy the odds, if you reach the prison, there's another ordeal to face." Aduro paused. "Grashkor the Beast Guard. He feeds his magic on the prisoners enslaved to him."

The name made Tom's skin feel cold. "A Beast?" he said.

Aduro nodded. "An Evil Beast. Perhaps the most vicious that the Kingdoms have ever known. He claimed the life of Ledrahon, one of the Masters of the Beasts before your father. It was only because Grashkor was weak from that fight that I was able to imprison him on the island. He's remained there ever since, alone with the prisoners kept in the Chamber of Pain.

But now… If Petra and Malvel are sending him new captives, there's a chance he may become hungry for more humans to keep in his grasp and fuel his magic. There's a chance he could attack Avantia! You have to go after Elenna – rescue her and defeat Grashkor for good."

Tom saw the door swing open as Aduro's magic released it. "May good fortune follow you."

Tom set off before first light, leading Storm by his reins so the stallion's hooves wouldn't wake the King's household. Aduro had told Tom his magic was too weak to deliver him directly to the Western shores – it wasn't just his crystal ball that Petra had tampered with. Tom had no choice, he had to ride to the shore.

Silver, recovered from his ordeal, sloped along beside Tom. Stars glittered in the sky as the palace guard waved them over the drawbridge. At Tom's waist hung a pouch of gold coins from Aduro.

"You won't find someone to take
you across the sea," he'd said, "but
at least you might be able to buy
a boat."

As Tom walked away from the city,

he felt a burden of guilt at leaving. King Hugo had deliberately left him behind so that if danger arose, Tom would be there to face it. But he was confident the recruits could manage under Captain Harkman's watchful eye.

He hadn't gone far when he heard the faint sound of footsteps some way behind. Tom quickened his steps, crossing a small stream. The footsteps quickened too.

Petra? he wondered. *Would she really dare to face me one on one?*

Rounding a curve in the road, Tom led Storm and Silver off the path and into some bushes. He stopped and waited.

Tom's pursuer was almost running to keep up. As they drew level, Tom leapt from behind the bush, drawing his sword and levelling the point a hair's breadth from the figure's back.

"Turn round and face me, Petra!" he demanded.

CHAPTER FOUR

HELP OR HINDRANCE?

The figure turned around slowly.
Sebastian stared at Tom, open-
mouthed. He was wearing a sword
and shield from the palace armoury.

"I didn't mean any... I didn't mean
to scare..." he stammered.

Tom sighed and lowered his sword.
"Why are you following me?"

Sebastian shrugged. "I saw you
saddling your horse in the stables,"

he said. "You must be going on an adventure, and I thought you'd need some help."

Tom clucked with his tongue and Storm and Silver came out of hiding. "Go back to the palace and go to bed," he told the boy.

Tom started off down the path again, but Sebastian caught up. "I know something's wrong," he said. "You never go anywhere without Elenna."

"Yes, something is very wrong," said Tom. "And that's why you mustn't follow me. The road ahead is dangerous."

Sebastian puffed out his chest. "You said I was a good fighter."

Tom stared at Sebastian, trying to think of a way to dissuade him. The boy's wide eyes held no fear and Tom

could sense courage in his heart.

He reminds me of someone… he
thought.

"All right," he said finally. "You can
come." Sebastian's face broke out in
a huge grin. "But," Tom added, "you
have to do exactly what I say. If I tell
you to get out of harm's way, you do
as I say. Understand?"

"Yes," said Sebastian. "And one
more thing?"

"What's that?" asked Tom.

Sebastian gave a cheeky smile. "Can I ride in front?"

It took them two days to reach the shore.

They took rest stops by the side of the path at night, but never for long. At last the scrub grass gave way to sand dunes and Tom smelt the scent of salty sea air. Topping a mound, Tom saw the expanse of ocean disappearing to the horizon. Under a slate grey sky, it didn't look at all inviting.

"We should dismount," Tom said.

They slipped off the saddle and Tom took the reins to lead Storm across the sand. His stallion snorted and stamped as they faced out to sea.

Silver ran around in bursts, forward and back, howling at the black chopping waves.

They can sense Elenna's out there somewhere, Tom thought. He patted Storm's muscular neck. "You have to stay here, old friend," he said. "You too, Silver," he said. The wolf sat patiently beside Storm's hooves, tongue lolling.

Tom set off along the beach with purposeful strides.

"Don't you need to tie them up?" asked Sebastian, looking back at the animals as he jogged beside Tom.

Tom shook his head. "They'll wait until we return," he said. "We need to find a boat as soon as possible."

It wasn't long before they came across a network of wooden walkways on the beach. At the

end of one, where the waves lapped
the sand, a white-bearded fisherman
was heaving a basket of fish from
a small boat.

"Hail there," called Tom. "We come
from King Hugo's city. We'd like to
borrow a boat."

"Borrow?" said the man, his eyes
narrowing in his weather-beaten
face. "You don't look much like
fishermen. How would I know
you'd bring it back?"

"I give you my word," said Tom.

"Your word means little to me,
young fellow," said the man. He
rubbed his finger and thumb
together. "I trust a different sort of
promise, if you know what I mean."

"How much?" said Tom, reaching
for his pouch.

The old man grinned. "The boat

will cost you twenty gold pieces."

Tom gulped as the old man continued unloading his catch. The boat's timbers were bleached by the sea. Its rudder was splintered and worn and it hadn't seen a coat of paint for years. It certainly wasn't worth twenty pieces – it probably wasn't worth half that. Tom scanned up and down the beach, but there weren't any other boats in sight. They might have to walk for hours before they found another.

And we don't know how long Elenna's got left, he thought.

Tom was reaching for his pouch when Sebastian stepped forward. "We'll give you five pieces of gold," he said, winking at Tom.

The fisherman straightened up and crossed his arms. "Know your boats, do you?" he said, waving his hand over his old vessel. "That's good quality timber, that is. Eighteen."

Sebastian put a hand on Tom's arm. "We should keep walking. He's trying to cheat us. That wreck will tip over in a strong tide."

"Fifteen!" said the fisherman.

"Five," said Sebastian.

"Twelve," said the fisherman. "I'm doing you a favour."

Sebastian made a show of looking over the boat from bow to stern. "Five."

The fisherman flapped his arms in disbelief. "Aren't you listening? Eleven."

Sebastian counted on his fingers, then said, "Five."

The fisherman sniffed. "Ten. Final offer."

"Nine," said Sebastian.

"Eight," said the fisherman.

"Done!" said Sebastian. "Eight gold pieces."

The old man slapped his forehead. "*Doh!* You made me count backwards. You tricked me!"

Tom smiled as he counted out the eight gold pieces and handed them to the fisherman. The old man

grumbled as he carried his baskets of
fish up the beach.

Tom was clambering into the boat
when a wet Silver splashed alongside
and jumped in too. Tom thought
about shooing him away, but
something made him stop. *He's*

Elenna's wolf, he thought. *Maybe he should come with us.*

"I thought you said he would stay put," said Sebastian.

Tom looked at the loyal friend. "Elenna might need him," he replied. "Come on. Let's get going!"

CHAPTER FIVE

THE CHAMBER OF PAIN

There was only a single set of oars, so Tom and Sebastian took one each and rowed together. They pulled quickly away from the shore with powerful strokes. Soon Tom could no longer see Storm or the fisherman. Breaking surf smashed over the prow of the boat, soaking them with spray.

Once they'd reached the long rolling waves out on the open water,

Sebastian helped him unfurl the sail. Tom took out his compass, and steered them towards the south-west as Aduro had instructed. The boat picked up speed as the sails filled and strained, making the small mast creak. Cold wind whipped through Tom's clothes and hair.

"Have you ever been this way before?" asked Sebastian, hugging himself for warmth.

"Never," said Tom, gazing out toward the horizon until his eyes hurt.

Who knows what creatures these dark seas conceal? Tom thought.

Clouds scudded across the gloomy sky as they sailed on. Occasionally shark fins broke the surface of the water, but they didn't seem interested in Tom's small craft.

"There!" shouted Sebastian suddenly. He pointed ahead and off to the left.

The pale haze of the horizon was broken by four massive square turrets rising above jagged battlements. Gulls swooped over the dark towers, and their shrill screeching reached Tom's ears like far-off misery.

"The Chamber of Pain," he murmured.

As they sailed closer, the prison grew in size. He'd never seen anything like it in Avantia. Grey walls, taller than those of King Hugo's castle, loomed over them, stained red and brown. Tom saw now that the birds weren't gulls at all. Their hooked beaks and long scrawny necks marked them out as vultures. Tiny slit windows looked out towards

the sea. Winds whistled along the
masonry and waves smashed into the
rocks of the island that sprouted

around the base of the fortress.

My friend's in there somewhere, Tom thought.

It wasn't until they were right at the base of the prison, where the sea water had coated the walls with streaks of green slime, that Tom saw a way in. Halfway along the wall a low opening gave way to the inside. Tom lowered the sail and guided the boat beneath the dark archway. As they drifted into the shadows, Tom cast a glance back towards the distant blur of Avantia's coastline. Would he ever see home again?

They found themselves in a cold black tunnel where the water slapped the walls. Silver whined, and the sound echoed back. The channel they were in grew narrower, so Tom could no longer extend the oars each side

of the boat. He and Sebastian pulled
themselves through the water by
gripping the rough stone of the walls.
As his eyes adjusted to the gloom,
they reached a sloping stone jetty
with embedded iron hoops as big as
his hand. Three doors led away from
the mooring place.

"This is where we stop," he said.

Tom climbed out of the boat, tying
it to one of the iron hoops with

a rope. Almost at once, he felt
a piercing pain inside his skull. Beside
him, Sebastian clutched his head and
fell to his knees with a cry.

"What's happening?" he gasped.

Tom helped his friend to his feet,
trying to ignore the stabbing agony in
his own brain. "This place is called
the Chamber of Pain for a reason."
He made Sebastian face him.
"Remember our training? In any
battle there are distractions. It might
be the weather, it might be the
terrain. This is just another
distraction. It's important to stay
focused on our enemy – Grashkor."

Gradually the pained grimace
creasing Sebastian's face vanished.
Whatever had attacked them was
fading away. Silver's paws pattered
on the stone as he disembarked too.

Tom led the way along the middle passage, squinting into the darkness and feeling the cold walls with his fingertips.

"We need to keep track of where we're going if we're to get out again," he whispered.

He drew his sword, bracing the point against the wall. As he walked he scraped a scar deep into the stone, throwing off occasional sparks that cast a dim glow over the way ahead. It might be all they had to guide themselves out again.

He saw dim light ahead and quickened his steps. He rounded a corner...

Tom stopped and threw out an arm to halt Sebastian. They stood at the edge of a wide dark pool, filling a vaulted cavern beyond. The water reflected blackly like a mirror. Hundreds of stepping stones, some wide as tree stumps, others half a handspan across, were dotted at intervals in the lake. Silver sniffed the water and looked up at Tom.

"Do we cross?" asked Sebastian. For the first time, he sounded nervous. Ahead, a stream of bubbles broke the surface. *Something lives in there*, Tom realised. He saw shapes flitting back and forth. "We have to," he said. With one hand still clutching the wall and the other on the hilt of his sword, he reached out a foot to the first stepping stone. Gradually, he let his weight rest on it. He let go of the wall and stepped to the next stepping stone. It began to sink, so Tom stepped hastily back.

"Not all of them are safe," he said

to Sebastian. "Make sure you follow my route exactly."

Tom picked his way across the stones. From time to time silvery flashes broke the surface. Swirls and ripples edged around the stepping stones, making his skin crawl.

If we fall in here, Tom thought, *we'll never reach dry land again.*

"Help!" called Sebastian.

Tom twisted round and saw Sebastian a few stones behind him, his arms wheeling as he tried to keep his balance. A fish the size of his hand had fastened dagger-like teeth into the cadet's trousers. *Piranhas!* Tom quickly unhooked his belt and held out his sheathed sword.

Sebastian managed to grab the tip of the blade to steady himself. The stubborn fish fell back into the water with a splash.

"Thanks!" gasped Sebastian.

Tom stared into the water with a shiver. So the pool was full of piranhas. He'd heard these deadly fish could strip a body of flesh in no time at all.

They set off again, and in three more steps Tom reached the far side of the pool. Sebastian followed. Both of them were sweating as they stood together. Only then did Tom see Silver still waiting at the far side, pacing back and forth.

I can't leave him there, Tom thought. "Come on!" he breathed. "You can do it!"

Silver's ear cocked. Edging closer to the water, he leapt onto the first stone, then without stopping, bounded to another, then another,

following Tom's route. Swarms of
ravenous fish streamed through the
water, tracking the wolf just in case
he fell. But Silver reached the other
side and stood panting.

"He made it look easy!" said
Sebastian.

Two narrow passages led from the
bank, further into the depths of the

fortress. Tom was just wondering which they should take when a clanking noise reached his ears. Silver growled. Tom stepped in front of Sebastian and drew his sword. The noises grew louder. It sounded like footsteps.

"Which tunnel is it coming from?" asked Sebastian, brandishing his blade.

Tom saw the shadows first and his throat went dry. "It's coming from both of them," he whispered.

CHAPTER SIX

THE DEATH GUARD

Two creatures stepped from the tunnels wearing stained leather straps over muscular bodies. Tom thought at first they might be giant men, but one look at their faces told him otherwise. They each had a single eye, high in their foreheads. *Cyclops!* Their heads were shaved, with only tufts of hair remaining, and they carried huge, broad-bladed swords.

The one nearest to Tom leered, showing a mouth full of rotten stumps where his teeth should be.

"Kill the intruders!" he roared.

Tom leapt forward, swinging his sword. The guard backed off into the tunnel. Tom swung again, but his blade slid harmlessly off the tough leathery skin.

Tom heard the clash of metal on metal as Sebastian fought their other foe. The Cyclops facing Tom swung his sword in a slashing movement, that would have cleaved Tom in two if he hadn't dodged sideways. With another vertical swipe, he drove Tom back. *He's used to fighting here*, Tom realised. He deflected an upward blow with his shield, but tripped backwards.

The giant raised his sword with

both hands to deliver the fatal chop.

Tom scrambled between his legs.
As the Cyclops turned, Tom rammed
his shield into his enemy's chin. The
giant's knees crumpled and he sagged
to the floor unconscious.

Tom ran quickly back to help
Sebastian. The other Cyclops

staggered backwards to the edge of the dark pool as Sebastian lunged at his chest. The cadet swiped again, clattering his enemy's sword into the water. Now Silver leapt up, snapping at the Cyclops's face. With a cry, the guard toppled back, splashing into the pool. Bubbles seethed as the piranhas swarmed over their victim, darting and snapping their razor-sharp jaws. Tom watched as the Cyclops writhed and struggled, then disappeared into the dark water. Only a tattered piece of leather floated up to the surface.

"Are you all right to go on?" Tom asked a pale-faced Sebastian. The boy nodded.

Tom frowned as he inspected the two tunnels. If they took the wrong passage, they may never find Elenna.

Silver scampered over the unconscious Cyclops, lifting his nose. He looked back at Tom and whined.

"I think he can smell Elenna!" said Tom.

"And it's the only clue we've got," said Sebastian.

They stepped over the Cyclops and followed Silver down the passage. Water dripped from the ceiling and occasional chill breezes tickled Tom's skin. He kept his sword drawn, and moved slowly, just in case they met any more one-eyed warriors.

Or something more deadly, Tom thought with a shudder.

Soon the passage emerged into a huge barren courtyard. Moss grew between uneven stone paving slabs, several paces across. Tom gazed up and saw four great towers pointing

skyward at each corner. Ramparts
joined them to one another on each
side, with open corridors exposed
to the elements.

"We're in the middle of the prison,"
he said. "Those are the four turrets
we could see from the outside."

Floor after floor of barred windows
climbed each tower, each one the
window to a cell. Tom's eyes darted,
searching for his friend.

"Tom!" called a voice he recognised.

Silver dashed past Tom's legs to the base of the tower directly ahead. He planted his paws on the stone as if he wanted to climb the sheer wall. Tom's eyes found a pale, bruised face several windows up.

"Elenna!" he shouted back as he jogged nearer.

Silver howled mournfully towards his mistress and the sound reverberated around the courtyard.

"Tom!" Elenna yelled. "You have to keep Silver quiet before…"

The sky suddenly darkened, and Tom looked up expecting to see a cloud passing over the faint disk of the sun.

There was no cloud.

A creature stood on the tallest rampart of the fortress. The Beast's barrel-like torso was something like a man's, but covered in grey-green scales. A silver helmet, stained with rust or blood, covered its head. Tom could barely see its face, because the long noseguard cast it in shadow, but two ice-blue eyes glowed. The Beast wore a tunic made of stitched animal hides, blackened by flame.

His long arms reached almost to the ground. His right hand unfurled a weapon that made Tom's stomach heave. Nine huge bones, bleached white in places with patches of rotting flesh in others, were linked with leather thongs to form a long whip. The final section that dangled lowest was a bull's skull, complete with curved horns.

"Grashkor!" breathed Tom.

"We'll fight him together," said

Sebastian with a tremor in his voice.

The Beast leapt from his perch. Tom thought it would fall, but the Death Guard spread two huge leathery wings stretched over a skeletal frame. For a moment he hovered, beating the air with his pinions.

Grashkor tipped one wing and swooped into the courtyard towards them, claws outstretched.

"Duck!" shouted Tom.

The Beast soared over their heads, roaring. "More prisoners at last!" he cried.

As Tom and Sebastian stood up again, the bone-chain was already looping towards them. There wasn't time to warn Sebastian. Tom shoved his companion hard and saw Sebastian stagger out of harm's way.

The bull's head mace slammed into Tom's chest with the force of a galloping horse. His feet left the floor and for a heartbeat he was sailing through the air. Then he smashed back onto the ground.

Tom lay still while the world span

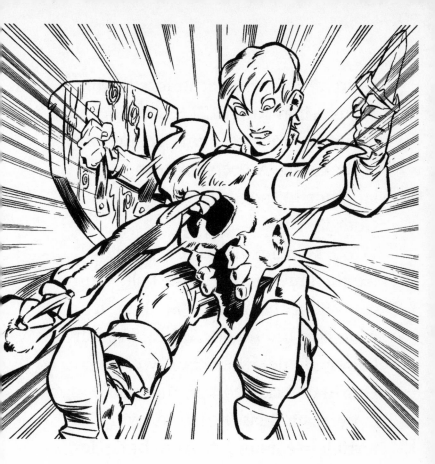

around him. His chest felt horribly tight and he couldn't draw breath. Shards of pain stabbed at his side.

My ribs are broken. I can't move, he thought.

The ground shook as Grashkor landed in the middle of the

courtyard, his powerful legs flexing as his wings furled. The Beast began to lumber towards him, trailing the bone-chain. A deep, growling laughter sounded from the Death Guard's throat.

Tom's fingers frantically searched for the green jewel in his belt. Won from Skor the Winged Stallion, it gave him the power to heal broken bones. He detached the jewel as Grashkor's clawed feet stamped closer. The Beast began to swing his terrible weapon, first in tight circles, then larger ones. The bull's head sailed round and round, gathering speed.

Tom held the jewel over his chest, feeling the magical warmth spreading across his broken bones. But it was too late. Grashkor's shadow fell

across him, and beneath the helmet
bloodless lips spread into a smile.
With a jerk of the Beast's arm, the
bull's head lashed towards Tom.

CHAPTER SEVEN

IMPRISONED

Sebastian let out a war-cry and leapt
in front of Tom, brandishing his
sword. His blade met the bone-chain
just beneath the bull's head,
showering them all with sparks.
Grashkor's arm jolted under the
force and the Beast staggered back,
spreading his wings and taking flight.

Tom felt his ribs stiffen and
strengthen as they knitted back
together. He managed to draw a huge

breath and rolled to his feet.

"You saved my life," he said to Sebastian.

"I told you I'd be able to help!" the boy replied.

Silver came towards them, yelping as Grashkor climbed, wheeling in the air for another strike.

Tom looked around desperately. His eyes lighted on a low wooden door at the base of the tower where Elenna was being held. The frame around it was made of linked shards of bone.

Grashkor let out a screeching cry as he fell from the sky towards them.

"This way," said Tom, grabbing Sebastian's arm and yanking him towards the tower. "We can't fight Grashkor in the open. We have to take shelter."

The Beast levelled off, swooping

over the courtyard at speed. Tom ran
for the door with the Death Guard
closing in on them. As he shouldered
the wooden panels, followed by
Sebastian and Silver, he thought he
heard Elenna call out, "No!"

They bundled through the door
into the base of the tower, landing in
a heap at the bottom of some spiral
steps. Outside, Grashkor's screech
turning to choked laughter.

Tom saw why. The bones fell away from the door-frame, and the wood seemed to fade. Patches of stone spread across the boards like flowing water. By the time Tom had leapt to his feet, the door was a bare wall. Tom ran his hands over the stone.

"This can't be..." he muttered.

"Magic," said Sebastian grimly. "A trap."

We're prisoners now, too, Tom thought. Aduro had warned Tom that Grashkor's power grew when more prisoners fell to him – and so did his hunger for even more victims. If Tom couldn't get out of here, with Elenna, he might be putting the whole Kingdom in danger.

Silver whined and faced the spiral stairs. *He wants to find Elenna*, Tom thought. *And so do I.*

He started to climb.

After a few steps, they reached a cell door, bracketed with steel hinges. The keyhole was empty. Tom barely paused – Elenna was at least twelve floors up. After another eleven steps was another door. He heard a scratching and muttering on the other side. Tom slowed, and put his ear to the door. Sebastian watched him, swallowing nervously. A man's voice repeated the same phrase, over and over. Tom finally picked up what he was saying.

"Once in, never out. Once in, never out. Once in…"

Tom jerked his ear away. "Once in, never out," he repeated. His heart felt as cold as ice. *How long has that poor man been imprisoned?* he wondered. *How long since he lost his mind?*

Sebastian banged a fist on the cell door. "Listen," he said. "We will get out of here!"

The voice on the other side broke into cackling laughter.

"Grashkor never releases a prisoner," said the man. "Even if you leave the Chamber of Pain, the Beast will pursue you to the ends of the world. Any kingdom you flee to, the Death Guard will follow. He will destroy all before him. Don't you understand: that is his curse!"

"We're wasting time," said Tom, pushing on up the stairs. But as he climbed, trying to drive the prisoner's words from his mind, they kept returning like an evil echo.

Tom's stomach churned to think of the Death Guard unleashed on the innocent kingdom of Avantia.

"I've been a fool!" he said aloud. "We should never have tried to escape Grashkor through that door."

"You couldn't let your friend rot in this place," said Sebastian.

Tom stopped and stared into his companion's eyes. In them he saw the reflection of his own haunted face.

"Malvel will stop at nothing to conquer Avantia," he said. "While there is blood in our veins we have to get Elenna out, and we have to stop Grashkor leaving this place!"

STORY TWO

I can't believe Tom would be so reckless! I tried to warn him. Sometimes he's too loyal for his own good. He should know by now, I'd give my life for the Kingdom, just as Tom would. And poor Silver might never recover from being on this wretched island.

Now, they face an impossible task. How can Tom rescue me, find a safe way out of this Chamber, and get off the island without risking the destruction of his beloved kingdom?

I fear Malvel has finally set the perfect trap.

Tom has not yet seen the full force of Grashkor's power and rage. This island holds many deadly dangers. They don't call this the Chamber of Pain for nothing.

Is this one Quest too far for my best friend?

Elenna

CHAPTER ONE

AERIAL ESCAPE

Silver shot up the steps. Tom took three steps at a time, using the magical power from Tagus's horseshoe in his shield to drive his feet faster.

"Wait for me!" called Sebastian.

Tom reached the heavy-timbered door at the top, and Sebastian came panting behind. Huge brass hinges hung at one side of the door, but there was no lock to break. Silver, on his hind legs, scraped at the wood with his front paws.

"Is that you, Silver?" came Elenna's voice from within.

"Hold on!" said Tom. "We'll get you out."

Tom ran at the door and pain exploded through his shoulder. The door didn't budge. Silver whined.

"I'll help," said Sebastian. Taking a step back, he aimed a kick at the edge of the door. The boy bounced backwards. Tom shouldered it again. And again. The door didn't even shake in its hinges.

From outside, Grashkor's muted roars of triumph reached Tom's ears. He sagged back beside Sebastian. *What if the prisoner's words were right? What if Grashkor has won and we're trapped forever?*

Sebastian had drawn his sword and was hacking at one of the hinges. Sparks scattered off, reflecting in the dark pools of Silver's eyes.

"Good idea!" said Tom. "Let's take it in turns."

He unsheathed his trusty blade and raised it above his head. As he brought it down, the hinge gave a dull clang that rattled through his bones. The metal plates shifted slightly on the door.

"It's working!" said Sebastian.

His next blow almost smashed the top hinge off the stone wall.

"One more," said Tom, hefting his sword. "Stand back, Elenna!"

The hinge broke free completely and the door leant slowly inwards, then tipped over, smashing to the ground inside the cell. Stale air wafted over Tom in a cloud of dust. Silver leapt into the room, barking excitedly.

Elenna, her hair matted and her face streaked with dirt, crouched and threw her arms around the wolf. The cell had bare stone walls, and a single narrow window with no glass. She looked thinner than the last time Tom had seen her, but her dark eyes were determined.

Detaching herself from Silver, she went to a corner of the room and

picked up her bow and arrow quiver.

"I'm surprised they let you keep
your weapons," said Sebastian.

"They're no use here," said Elenna.
"I think Malvel wanted to taunt me."

Tom looked proudly at his friend.
Even after all she'd been through,
she still wanted to fight.

"We'll make him pay for his

mistake," Elenna said. She walked towards the broken door, but Tom shook his head. "There's no way out down there. The door at the bottom has disappeared." He nodded towards the window. "That's our escape route."

Sebastian's eyes widened with alarm. "We can fit through one by one, but unless we sprout wings, it's a long drop to the bottom!"

Tom grinned, then rolled his shield onto his arm and thumped the surface. "We haven't got wings, but this is the next best thing. Arcta's feather will slow our fall."

Together they made their way to the window. Tom peered out into the courtyard below where they'd faced Grashkor. There was no sign of the Death Guard, even though they'd heard his roars only moments ago. A vulture wheeled in the sky above the turret, gazing down at them hungrily.

"Tom," said Elenna, "are you sure the eagle feather will support all four of us?"

No, I'm not! Tom thought, *but it's our only hope.*

"Trust me," he said.

Elenna nodded and Tom climbed out onto the narrow ledge.

Tom heard Sebastian gasp as he threw himself into the air, shield aloft, calling on the power of Arcta to help him hover. Wind whipped around his clothes, and he stared over the battlements out to the black sea beyond.

"You next, Sebastian," he said. "You need to take my waist."

The boy clambered gingerly onto

the ledge. His face was pale, but his eyes remained focused. Getting his balance, he leapt away from the tower. Tom felt hands clutch his tunic and belt. For a moment, they wobbled in the air, but Tom closed

his eyes and concentrated, keeping them steady.

Now for the hard bit, he thought.

Elenna inched out of the window, crouching on the sill. Silver hopped up beside her and looked uncertainly from the courtyard to his mistress. She wrapped one arm around Silver's middle and pulled him tightly towards her.

"You can do it," said Tom. "Just take hold of Sebastian's belt."

Elenna muttered something under her breath and leant out, reaching with her one free hand. She caught hold of the belt.

Tom knew at once that he couldn't hold the weight. One sweating palm slipped free of the shield and they plummeted towards the ground. Elenna's screams mingled with

Sebastian's shouts and Silver's howls. Tom gritted his teeth and tried to grasp the shield with his free hand. He missed. The prison walls became a blur. Tom's shield fell beside them and he reached again. This time he managed to snatch the shield's edge and clung on. His arms and shoulders burned as he tried to keep them steady. Gradually their descent slowed and the rushing ground drifted towards them.

We're going to be all right, he thought.

When Elenna was nearly touching the stone flags, she suddenly jerked to a stop in mid-air. Tom's shoulder was nearly pulled from its socket and he had to bite his lip not to scream with pain. A wave of foul breath filled his nostrils. He looked up.

Above them, clutching the shield
with one huge hand, was the
Death Guard.

CHAPTER TWO

A BRAVE SACRIFICE

Grashkor's wings beat the air as he
hovered above them. With a flick
of his wrist, the Beast jolted them
higher. The Death Guard's blue eyes
flared under his stained helmet, and
from his other arm he let the bone-
whip unfurl. The bull's skull *thunked*
onto the stone pavings.

"Let go!" shouted Tom to Sebastian.
"He'll kill us all if you don't!"

He felt Sebastian's grip loosen and

the boy and Elenna landed in a heap below. Tom was glad to see them find their feet quickly. He struggled to yank his shield from the Beast's grip, but couldn't. So he let go – leaving the Beast holding his shield – and dropped. As soon as he hit the ground, he heard the air whistle and the bone chain snaked around his legs. He felt himself upended and flung high into the air as though he weighed nothing.

He slammed onto the ground and rolled onto his back. The bone-whip loosened then rattled away. The skies darkened above Tom and seemed to spin, but he managed to climb woozily to his feet and fell against a wall. Grashkor had tossed him right across the courtyard.

"Don't give up!" shouted a man's voice. In the tower above, a thin face pressed between the bars of a window. Other prisoners appeared at the windows, most faces matted with long beards, and covered in filthy smears. "Kill the Beast!" they shouted, and "Take heart!". Others merely looked on in silent astonishment.

The poor souls are trapped here, Tom thought.

The Beast, with hideous wings

spread, swooped down upon Elenna and swung the deadly chain. It snapped through the air towards Tom's friend, but she stepped nimbly aside. As she dodged, she grabbed the eye-socket of the skull as it passed. The whip's momentum jerked her body off the ground and carried her up in an arc. She leapt off and landed right on Grashkor's shoulder at the edge of his wing. Tom, still recovering from his fall, felt his mouth drop open in astonishment at the feat. Elenna was struggling to stay balanced as she drew an arrow from her quiver.

Sebastian dived between the Beast's clawed legs and hacked at the curved talons. Grashkor roared as he fell to his knees, his wings flapping madly. Just as Elenna strung an arrow and

took aim, Tom saw the Beast reach
up to grab her.

"Look out!" Tom called.

Elenna's head jerked round. She
leapt off the armoured shoulder, her
arrow veering aimlessly, and tumbled

across the Beast's wing. Grashkor's
fist collided into his own face and he
staggered sideways.

Tom ran forwards, snatching up his
fallen shield and drawing his sword.

It's time to end this, he thought, as
he joined his brave companions.

Grashkor steadied himself, his claws
cutting gouges in the stone. He
lurched around to face them and
shook his helmeted head as if to clear
it. His wings closed behind his back
and he gripped the whip, one end
in each fist, and pulled it tight.

"After you are dead," he growled,
"Avantia will fall!"

The words shook Tom's bones.
He stayed in front of the others, but
together they backed off towards the
corner of the courtyard. On the
opposite side, Tom spied the archway

by which they'd entered. Grashkor
stalked after them, grinning.

"If we can get into the tunnels,"
said Elenna. "Grashkor will be too
big to follow."

"He's got the advantage in the
open," said Sebastian. "He can pick
us off one by one."

But if we flee, thought Tom, *there'll*

be nothing to stop Grashkor flying to
Avantia. I'll have failed. Unless…
Would Aduro be able to help?

Sebastian came to Tom's side as
Grashkor let the whip swing back
and forth menacingly. "I'll distract
him and you run for it," he said.

"I can't ask you to cover for us,"
said Tom. "You might be killed."

"You're not asking me to do
anything," said Sebastian, "I'm
volunteering. You know how quick
I am – I'm quick enough to keep
Grashkor busy. I'll be right behind
you."

Tom knew the boy was right. He
was quick – Tom remembered from
their sparring sessions. *But can I leave*
a boy to battle with a Beast?

"Please," said Sebastian, "let me
do this for Avantia."

His words touched Tom's heart. If they managed to get back to Avantia, they could use Aduro's magic to help defeat Grashkor. He clapped the boy on the shoulder. "We'll wait by the boat."

Sebastian lifted his sword and ran at Grashkor with a cry: "For Avantia!"

CHAPTER THREE

ACT OF DESTRUCTION

As Sebastian ran at Grashkor, the Beast bellowed and reached with one long clawed arm to snatch up the boy. Sebastian jumped over the sweeping hand and darted between Grashkor's legs.

"Catch me if you can!" shouted the cadet.

As soon as the Beast turned, Tom and Elenna broke into a run. Silver streaked along beside them. From the corner of his eye, Tom saw Grashkor push off the ground above Sebastian's swinging sword. Tom reached the archway to the tunnels, letting Elenna and Silver pass into the darkness in front of him.

Sebastian was busy slashing at the Beast's wings, while Grashkor threatened with his bone-whip. *Good luck!* Tom willed his companion, then plunged after Elenna.

As they threaded through the semi-darkness of the tunnels, Grashkor's angry roars echoed after them. Tom heard the clang of metal as Sebastian's sword found its target and the thud of the bone-whip meeting stone. They tore on as quickly as they could, rounding corner after corner. Tom's eyes strained against the gloom, half-expecting more of the Cyclops guards to block their path.

"Wait a moment," said Elenna.

Tom stalled, and looked back at his friend. Silver stood a few paces further back, sniffing the air.

"What's the matter with him?" asked Tom.

"I don't know," said Elenna. She stroked the wolf's grey fur. "He must sense danger."

"We have to press on," said Tom.

Elenna nodded, but she was frowning at the same time.

"Come on, boy," she muttered.

As they continued through the tunnels, odd grinding sounds echoed after them. Every few steps dust scattered from the roof. Tom hardly recognised the route they were taking, but he recognised his sword gouges on the wall. The sounds of the battle were fading behind them.

"This isn't right," said Elenna. "This route is going uphill."

Tom stopped again. *She's right*, he thought, examining the track. *The way to the boat should be downhill.*

Also, they hadn't passed the pool with the stepping stones, or the Cyclops he'd knocked out.

"I don't understand," Tom said. "We haven't missed any turnings. We must have come this way before."

At a slow walk, he carried on further until he saw a faint light ahead. "This way!" he called back.

But as the light grew brighter, he realised something was wrong. It wasn't the cavern where they'd left the boat.

Daylight!

A gusting wind buffeted his face. They'd emerged from the mouth of the tunnel onto a low clifftop. The sea smashed against the rocky shoreline below, and behind them loomed the great turrets of the Chamber of Pain. The Avantian coastline was nowhere to be seen.

"We're on the wrong side of the island!" Tom gasped.

Elenna ran a hand through her hair. "Evil magic is at work," she said. "That's why we heard those noises and saw dust fall from the cracks. The tunnels were moving. It must be

a trick to stop people from escaping!"

Tom felt despair creep over him,
but he shook it away. "We need to
follow the coastline around to the
boat," he said. "It's the only way
we'll find it again."

Elenna glanced towards the
wind-swept rocks, lashed by the
angry sea, and nodded. "Let's go."

They scrambled down towards the

shoreline, clambering over slippery boulders. Tom's anxiety deepened. What if the tunnels moved again? Sebastian would be trapped too! *We won't leave without him*, Tom thought grimly.

Pools of stagnant water were dotted between the rocks. Silver had no problems keeping his balance on four paws, leaping from one boulder to the next. Tom skinned his knuckles and knees several times crawling over the slime-covered stones. Gales blasted his body, threatening to topple him into the sea.

Malvel won't win! Tom promised himself.

His heart lifted when he recognised the side of the fortress they'd approached earlier, stained with filth. "We're almost at the boat entrance!"

he shouted to Elenna. Sure enough, the dark archway through which he'd guided the vessel came into view. "We'll have to swim inside to get the boat," he said to Elenna. "Do you think you can manage?"

"I didn't come this far to turn back," Elenna said. "Silver isn't afraid of water eith—"

A great roar cut off Elenna's words. Grashkor soared up from amid the prison towers, heading for the bruised clouds. His wings flashed back and forth, driven by powerful muscles, and his helmet glinted.

"Where's his whip?" Tom wondered aloud.

The clouds swallowed the Beast and he disappeared from view.

"I don't like it," said Elenna. "Grashkor didn't look injured."

"Perhaps Sebastian fought him off,"
said Tom hopefully. "All we can do
is wait."

A screech split the air, and like
a diving falcon, the Beast ripped back

through the clouds. His claws and wings were tucked in for extra speed as he dropped towards the Chamber of Pain at breakneck speed.

He's not going to stop! Tom thought.

A heartbeat after the Beast disappeared behind the walls the ground shook, almost knocking Tom to his knees. A roar like thunder rumbled through the rocks and the whole island juddered and seemed to tilt to one side.

"I don't believe it. He's trying to destroy the whole island!" cried Elenna.

CHAPTER FOUR

INTO THE JAWS OF DANGER

As Tom clung to a rock, the rasping voice of the prisoner returned to his thoughts. *Once in, never out. Once in...* Could Sebastian have survived the dive-bombing Beast?

"Grashkor won't let anyone leave," Tom said. "His powers are strengthened by keeping people captive. He'd rather sink the prison than lose his strength!"

"What shall we do?" asked Elenna. "We can't leave Sebastian."

If he's even still alive, thought Tom.

"We stick with our plan," said Tom, lowering himself into the freezing water. "We find the boat, then you head back to Avantia to warn Aduro. I'll follow the tunnels back and help tackle Grashkor."

Elenna jumped off the rock and splashed into the sea next to Tom. Silver joined them, diving and bobbing up alongside Elenna with his fur slicked back.

Together they swam through the archway. The island trembled and cracks opened up in the cavern roof over their heads. Rocks plummeted into the water. They found the boat safely moored at the jetty. Tom was climbing out when the island shook

again and the whole cavern lurched
to one side. Rocks and rubble cracked
off the walls, throwing up spouts of
water. *Grashkor's making another
assault*, he realised.

With water rising around his ankles
and threatening to swamp the jetty,
Tom unhooked the mooring rope.
"You need to hurry," he said, as
Elenna helped the drenched Silver
into the small vessel. "The cavern

won't hold for long."

Elenna pulled herself on board. Tom unhooked his shield and handed it across to her. "Take this," he said. "We saw sharks earlier and you might need Sepron's help on the open sea. Remember, the Serpent's Tooth in the shield will call him to you."

Elenna gazed at the shield as she took it. "Are you sure? How will you face the Death Guard without it?"

"I still have this," Tom said, patting his sheathed sword. He pushed the boat away before Elenna could argue. "If I don't see you again by nightfall," he said, "tell Aduro that Grashkor is coming to Avantia. Tell him I did my best."

"Good luck," said Elenna, her lips set in a grim line.

She stowed the shield under one

of the benches and took one oar, using it to push against the crumbling walls towards the entrance to the cave. Silver shook the water from his sodden fur and howled.

As the boat vanished around a corner and into the open sea, Tom turned and faced the three passages. Water was already flooding into them as the island broke apart around him. Last time Tom had taken the centre passage, but that was no guarantee it would lead the same way a second time. *I'll have to chance it*, he thought.

He raced back through the middle tunnel with water sloshing over his boots. The tunnel walls rumbled and juddered once more as Grashkor slammed into the island. A moment later Tom heard the rush of water at his back. He spun around and saw

a wall of white-foamed water surge
into the passage.

The sea's flooding the tunnel!

He took a deep breath as the tide
snatched him up and drove him
violently forwards.

For a moment, all he could see
were bubbles. Jolts of pain flared
through his body as he slammed into

the walls, the ground, the roof. He couldn't do a thing. He rolled over, grazing his back on rock, then curled into a ball to protect his head. He couldn't even call on the power of Sepron's fang to protect him from drowning, because the token was embedded in his shield.

Tom opened his eyes as the water released its grip. He floated upwards, found a pocket of air, and sucked in a breath, then dived. The tunnel looked different submerged, but he swam with powerful strokes through the flood. Seaweed floated in the water and piranhas flashed past in confused shoals. *They're not interested in me now*, Tom realised. He knew he was going the right way, because the tunnel was climbing, up towards the central prison.

As he rose to take a breath again, Tom jolted in shock as his head struck the ceiling. This time there was no air pocket – the passage was completely flooded! He pushed on, chest burning as his heart thumped under his ribcage. The quicker he reached the Chamber of Pain, the sooner he could take a breath.

Unless my breath runs out first...

An arm fell across Tom's face. He jerked back, flailing for his sword, but he saw at once that the limb held no threat. It was the body of the Cyclops guard, drifting gently through the water.

Tom pushed the body aside and kicked on, his lungs close to giving in. As his arms and legs worked, black spots dotted in his vision.

Not much further! he thought. *I can't*

stop now. Sebastian's relying on me.
I can't let Avantia down…

With a heaving gasp, his head broke the surface.

Tom sucked in breaths that felt like fire in his throat and lungs, then dragged himself through the water, chest-deep at first, then dropping to his waist. He stepped out of the seawater, soaked to his skin. Ahead of him he saw the courtyard of the Chamber of Pain, but it had

completely changed.

The whole prison leant at an angle, like the deck of a giant ship floundering at sea. Two of the turrets had already collapsed, leaving stumps of broken rubble. With a grinding sound that seemed to shake Tom's bones, the Chamber of Pain continued to tip, lurching ever more steeply to one side. Ankle-deep waves sloshed over the ancient paving stones, smacking against the walls, and massive stones broke off from the walls and plummeted into the swirling black water.

It's not just sinking, Tom realised. *It's capsizing!*

Grashkor swept in and out between the turrets, surveying his destruction and roaring in triumph.

"Tom!" shouted a voice.

Over the din of the toppling
masonry, and the smacking, rushing
water, Tom turned his head to the
sound. On the nearest of the
collapsed turrets, clinging to broken
rocks, stood Sebastian.

CHAPTER FIVE

A WATERY GRAVE

Tom didn't think Grashkor had seen him yet. The Beast rocked back on his wings beside the tower where Elenna had been imprisoned. He held his bone-whip once more. With a flick of his wrist, he lashed the turret, smashing through the stone and sending blocks out into the ocean. Hovering, the Death Guard gripped the remains with his claws and tore at the stone. There was no sign of any of the prisoners, but they couldn't possibly have survived such an assault.

No one deserves to die like that, Tom thought, *whatever is it they did wrong*.

While Grashkor was still busy pulling the fortress to pieces, Tom dashed across to the tower where Sebastian waited. Despite his weary limbs, he jumped from stone to stone

until he'd climbed to the boy's side. Sebastian's head was bleeding from a cut.

"I thought I could fight him…" said Sebastian, lowering his eyes in shame, "but he was too strong for me. I had to take shelter in the tower. There was nowhere else to go…"

"You did the right thing," said Tom. "Elenna is on her way to Avantia to warn Aduro. It's up to us to keep Grashkor here, if we can."

Across the courtyard, the Beast hovered as the third tower crumbled in a thunder of rubble and great clouds of dust.

"He doesn't seem interested in fighting us," said Sebastian.

"That's because if he destroys the island, he won't have to," said Tom.

"But I don't want to die today. Can you fight on?"

Sebastian drew his sword and Tom saw the blade was dented and nicked. "You fought bravely," Tom said.

"And I haven't finished yet," said Sebastian. He lifted the sword and pointed it at the Beast. "Over here, Grashkor!"

The Death Guard twisted in the air. As his pale eyes settled upon Tom and his companion, the Beast's chest heaved beneath his armour of fire-hardened leather. His bellow shook free more shifting stones. Grashkor dipped his head and dived.

Tom felt defenceless without his shield. Behind him the sea chopped and frothed beneath the fallen walls some twenty paces below. Grashkor shot through the air towards them.

Tom drew his sword, steadied himself, and lifted it with both hands, ready to strike at the Beast's helmeted head.

"If Grashkor crashes into us, at least we can take him with us," he said.

At twenty paces distance, the Beast swerved, and Tom saw the bull's skull whip lash around. It crunched into the base of the tower. Grashkor sailed past, shrieking with laughter as the

remains of the turret lurched and broke apart. Tom felt the ground beneath his feet quiver and buck. There were only two choices – to fall among the ruins, or take their chances in the water.

He grabbed Sebastian with his free hand and jumped towards the sea.

Tom heard the boy's cry of fear as they plummeted, legs wheeling through the air. The water snatched them under, but Tom kept hold of Sebastian, hooking his hand under the boy's armpit and paddling desperately towards the surface. He broke through, managed to sheath his sword, and dragged Sebastian up too. The boy was spluttering and scrambling in panic.

"It's all right," Tom said. "We're still alive!"

The walls and turrets of the Chamber of Pain continued to crumble, throwing up huge curtains of water. Waves rolled beneath Tom and Sebastian, lifting them to peaks and dropping them into troughs.

153

Grashkor hadn't yet emerged from the prison. *He probably thinks we're dead*, thought Tom.

"Er...is that what I think it is?" asked Sebastian.

Tom looked where the boy was pointing and felt his stomach turn over. Not far off, a triangular black fin sliced up through the water, then vanished.

"Sharks," said Tom, grimly. His hand found the hilt of his sword.

As they rose up on a wave, Tom sighted the fishing vessel in the distance. He couldn't tell if Elenna was looking their way or not, but he doubted he or Sebastian had the strength to swim that far anyway. The sharks, or the cold, would get them first.

"Bash the sharks on the nose with

your blade," Tom said. "Try not to
draw blood – it'll just attract more."

A dark shape approached. Tom
swung his sword and the shark
jerked away. His shoulders ached
already, and he knew he couldn't
hold them off for long. He heard
Sebastian grunt with effort as he
fought another stalking predator.

Then the boy shouted: "Oh no!
It's Grashkor!"

Sailing above them, the Death Guard circled on lazy wings. His eyes were fixed on the patch of water where Tom and Sebastian floated. Dipping slightly, he drifted closer in a swirling descent.

"He knows there's no rush," said Sebastian. "If he doesn't get us, the sharks will."

Tom struck another shark across its pointed nose, but he saw more fins edging through the waves.

Grashkor hovered right above them and unfurled his chain of bone. There was no way Tom or Sebastian could reach him with their blades. *No way even to defend ourselves*, Tom thought angrily.

The Beast gave a booming laugh as he lifted his arm to swing the deadly weapon.

"I'm sorry I got you into this," said Tom to his new friend.

"It was my choice," Sebastian replied. "At least it will be a quicker death than being eaten by sharks."

The bone-whip lashed around and the bull's head descended towards them. Its empty sockets stared right into Tom's heart and its bony jaws seemed to smile.

This is it, Tom thought. *This is where it ends.*

CHAPTER SIX

RESCUE FROM THE DEEP

A shower of water broke over them as something shot from the waves at their side. For a moment Tom thought it was a shark, but scales of every colour filled his vision. It looked like a rainbow bursting from the sea.

Sebastian gasped. Tom recognised the green-finned head. Jaws angled open and curved fangs closed over

the bone-whip, breaking it in two.

"Sepron!" Tom cried.

The bull's skull plopped harmlessly

into the sea a few paces away and sank out of sight. The remains of the chain of bones swung round and thumped into Grashkor's armoured chest. The Death Guard roared in pain and confusion as Sepron plunged beneath the waves again.

"What was that thing?" spluttered Sebastian.

"A loyal friend," said Tom.

The Sea Serpent emerged, fifty paces from where he'd dived. His body arced out of the water, driven by his powerful tail muscles. He snapped his jaws just a hand's breadth from Grashkor's dangling legs. The Death Guard lurched backwards and out of range.

The sharks around Tom and Sebastian had vanished. Sepron wound his long, glittering serpent's body around the boys in a protective loop. His pale eyes watched the skies.

Tom looked up. Grashkor cast away his whip among the ruins of the Chamber of Pain and raked the air with his claws. He growled. Beneath his helmet, his blue eyes flashed.

"He's not finished yet, is he?" said Sebastian. Tom saw his friend's lips were turning blue with cold.

High in the air, Grashkor folded his wings close to his body and rolled forwards into a dive. At the same time, Sepron slipped beneath the water. Tom saw his rainbow scales vanish into the depths at speed.

"What's he doing?" asked Sebastian. "Why's he leaving us?"

"I don't think he is," said Tom. The Death Guard dropped like a stone, his helmeted head angled to smash

anything in his path. Then Tom saw
Sepron surging up through the water.
*They're on a collision course! I can't let it
happen. Sepron's skull will be crushed!*
he thought.

Tom dipped his head beneath the water and waved his arms towards the climbing Beast, but the Sea Serpent didn't seem to notice. Tom came up again and saw Grashkor closing. He pushed Sebastian away and waved his arms. He'd rather give his own life than watch Sepron killed. "Come and get me, you big brute!" he yelled.

But Grashkor didn't change course. Tom was powerless to stop him. He closed his eyes as Grashkor plummeted towards the Good Beast.

Sudden heat blasted over Tom's face. He opened his eyes again as a ball of fire exploded over Grashkor's body. The Death Guard shrieked and veered off course, smashing into the water in a tangle of fire and twisted limbs.

Gleaming golden wings soared overhead and Tom saw bronze talons trailing flame.

"That bird just shot a fireball!" Sebastian yelled.

"Sebastian, meet Epos," said Tom, punching the air in triumph.

The Flame Bird swooped low, dipping her hissing talons into the icy water.

Tom was about to call back when

he felt his body jerked out of the water and thrown through the air. Epos's beak threw him backwards and he landed on a hard, ridge of black scales. Two skeletal wings, with a span over forty or fifty paces, heaved up and down on either side. Tom was breathless with shock as Ferno turned his head sideways and blinked a red eye in greeting.

As the wind blasted through his clothes and hair, Tom realised who he had to thank. "Elenna called you all, didn't she?" he shouted.

Ferno breathed a spurt of fire from his flexing jaws and tipped one wing. They sailed back towards where Sebastian remained in the water. "Hold on!" Tom called.

Ferno dipped again, and Tom heard a cry of alarm before Sebastian was

deposited behind him on the dragon's
back. The boy gripped Tom's waist.

"This is better than any horse ride!"
he yelled over the rushing wind.

The Beast looped up and carried
them high over the remains of the
prison island towards Elenna's boat.
Only a single tower remained, but
even that leant precariously. Water
surged through gaps in the walls and
the central courtyard was a seething

lake of filthy water. Tom saw it was
only a matter of time before the sea
claimed the Chamber of Pain
completely.

A screech from Epos made Ferno
swing suddenly around and Tom saw
what had alarmed the Flame Bird.
On a patch of sinking rock, a clawed
hand was reaching from the water.

Another followed as Grashkor unfolded his body from the sea.

"How do we defeat that thing?" cried Sebastian.

The Evil Beast shook water from its wings and flapped them twice, jumping skyward. The Beast's helmet had fallen away in the water, revealing a wide face of bone and rotting scraps of flesh. Tom felt a stab of pity for the wretched creature. Its armour was hanging off in patches as it flew towards the prison that had once been its home – and towards Elenna's boat.

Tom's pity vanished. He knew at once that the Death Guard was planning his final revenge.

He steered Ferno directly at the Beast. At the same time, he used the ruby in his belt, a token won from

Torgor the Minotaur, to communicate a message to Epos: *Be ready at the last tower!*

The Flame Bird screeched in understanding as Ferno bore down on Grashkor. If Tom timed it right, they should meet over the prison courtyard.

"What are you doing?" asked Sebastian. "We'll fly right into him!"

"Trust me!" said Tom, drawing his sword.

Just before they met, Tom tugged on one side of Ferno's neck and the Fire Dragon tipped side on. Tom leant out and raked his sword across Grashkor's wing, cutting a deep gash. The Evil Beast howled and dropped, spinning aimlessly into the midst of the submerged courtyard between the four ruined towers. As he hit the

water, it enclosed his body in bursts of spray. The Death Guard thrashed wildly, trying to right himself, but with only one working wing he was trapped.

"Now!" Tom shouted towards Epos.

The phoenix hurled a ball of flame towards the remaining turret. Fire engulfed the stone. As Ferno turned to the prison again, Tom watched the

tower tip inwards. Grashkor shrieked
as huge stones toppled towards him.
Then his cries were cut short. The

Death Guard was finished.

Tom didn't have time for pity. "Take us to Elenna!" he cried to Ferno.

CHAPTER SEVEN

AN ENEMY IN WAITING

Ferno hovered over the boat while
Tom and Sebastian carefully climbed
down. Silver gambolled happily as
they settled beside him. Ferno jerked
upwards with a few sweeps of his
wings and circled beside Epos.
Sepron's head broke the water
soundlessly beside the boat.

"You saved our lives," Sebastian
said to Elenna.

"For a time," Elenna replied, "I wasn't sure if either of you would make it out alive."

"I thought you might summon one Beast, but not three!" said Tom.

Sepron spouted water from his mouth.

"I think they're saying goodbye," said Elenna.

"Thanks, old friends," said Tom, raising his hand.

The Sea Serpent dipped his head, and with a great roll of his tail, sank away from sight. Ferno roared and puffed smoke from his jaws. He swept low over the boat and headed north. And last of all Epos tipped her golden beak in farewell and soared towards the setting sun.

"So the Good Beasts really do exist," said Sebastian. "No one back

at the castle will believe any of this!"
Tom looked sternly at his brave
young friend. "You mustn't tell them.

The Beasts are Avantia's secret. If everyone knows, they will be less able to defend the kingdom."

"Of course," said Sebastian, suddenly serious.

Tom took the oars, and began to row back towards the shore. The evening sea was calm, and looking back he saw the last of the island fortress disappear beneath the waves. "All those prisoners died too," said Tom. "I should have saved them."

"You couldn't have," said Elenna. "The important thing is that Grashkor's gone forever."

"I'm afraid that isn't true," said a voice.

Silver yipped and Tom almost dropped the oars as a vision appeared on the bench opposite, sitting between Elenna and Sebastian.

"Aduro!" said Elenna.

"This day's getting stranger and stranger," said Sebastian, rubbing his eyes.

The Wizard smiled. "My magic is working once more, which means Petra and Malvel's influence has been defeated. Congratulations, all of you!"

Tom flushed with pride. "What did you mean by what you said?" he asked. "Grashkor couldn't have survived, could he?"

"Grashkor will reappear," said Aduro grimly, "as will the prison and its prisoners. They are all cursed."

"I'm glad that I wasn't responsible for their deaths," said Tom, "but I hope I never have to fight Grashkor again."

"I hope not, too," said Aduro. "For now, I bid you the kingdom's thanks. Without you, Grashkor could have destroyed Avantia."

"What about the Barbarians?" asked Elenna.

"Defeated by King Hugo's army," said Aduro. "The kingdom is at peace once more. So for now, farewell, young heroes. I will see you at the Palace!"

The vision faded, leaving them alone in the boat once more.

The weariness seemed to fall from Tom's arms and he pulled the oars harder than ever. Soon they saw the shoreline approaching. A man sat on the sand, smoking a pipe. He wandered over as they pulled up in the shallows and Tom saw it was the fisherman who'd sold them the boat.

The old man's face creased in a frown. "Well, that's the strangest fishing trip I've ever seen. You haven't got any fish, yet you've managed to catch a girl and a dog!"

Silver growled.

"A wolf," Elenna corrected.

Tom dragged the boat onto the sand. "You can have the boat back, if you'd like."

The man puffed on his pipe. "And will you be wanting your seven gold pieces?"

"Eight," Sebastian reminded him. He grinned at Tom then turned back to the fisherman. "No, you can keep those. This little boat's done us proud."

They found Storm waiting patiently at the top of the dunes. He whickered happily to see his master safe. Tom helped Elenna into the saddle. "You climb on too," he said to Sebastian." I need to get my land legs back!"

As they trotted and walked away from the shore, night fell over the kingdom. They entered a forest path and a warm breeze whispered through the trees. For a fleeting moment, Tom thought it spoke to him: *"Once in, never out."*

He stopped and clutched Storm's

reins. "Did you hear that?" he asked his companions.

"Hear what?" said Sebastian.

Tom listened carefully, but now he only heard the wind.

"Silver doesn't seem worried," said Elenna. "His ears are better than all of ours combined."

"Ignore me," said Tom, pressing on. "It's been a long day."

The feeling of unease stayed with him. Even though Malvel was trapped in Gorgonia, Tom knew his magic rarely stopped at the borders of kingdoms.

But Avantia's safe for now. That's all that matters, he reassured himself.

Sebastian's voice broke in on his thoughts. "I've been thinking," he said. "Does this mean I can come on all your adventures?"

Tom glanced at Elenna and rolled his eyes. "Avantia needs you in the army," he said. "You're a fine soldier."

Sebastian grinned. "Well, I had a good teacher."

Tom looked to the road ahead and smiled. Perhaps he had trained Sebastian well, but with Malvel and Petra lurking around, he wouldn't have time for much more teaching.

Evil will never rest, he thought, *and we will always be ready.*

JOIN TOM ON HIS NEXT BEAST QUEST SOON!

Win an exclusive
Beast Quest T-shirt and goody bag!

Tom has battled many fearsome Beasts and we want to know which one is your favourite! Send us a drawing or painting of your favourite Beast and tell us in 30 words why you think it's the best.

Each month we will select **three** winners to receive a Beast Quest T-shirt and goody bag!

Send your entry on a postcard to
BEAST QUEST COMPETITION
Orchard Books, 338 Euston Road, London NW1 3BH.

Australian readers should email:
childrens.books@hachette.com.au

New Zealand readers should write to:
Beast Quest Competition, PO Box 3255, Shortland St,
Auckland 1140, NZ or email: childrensbooks@hachette.co.nz

Don't forget to include your name and address.
Only one entry per child.

Good luck!

All books priced at £4.99,
special bumper editions
priced at £5.99.

Orchard Books are available from all good bookshops, or can
be ordered from our website: www.orchardbooks.co.uk,
or telephone 01235 827702, or fax 01235 8227703.

Series 10: MASTER OF THE BEASTS
COLLECT THEM ALL!

An old enemy has come back to haunt Tom –
and unleash six awesome new Beasts!

978 1 40831 518 7

978 1 40831 519 4

978 1 40831 520 0

978 1 40831 521 7

978 1 40831 522 4

978 1 40831 523 1

Series 11: THE NEW AGE

Meet six terrifying new Beasts!

Elko Lord of the Sea
Tarrok the Blood Spike
Brutus the Hound of Horror
Flaymar the Scorched Blaze
Serpio the Slithering Shadow
Tauron the Pounding Fury

Watch out for the next
Special Bumper
Edition

The Chronicles of Avantia

FROM THE DARK, A HERO ARISES...

Dare to enter the kingdom of Avantia.

A new evil arises in Avantia. Lord Derthsin has ordered his armies into the four corners of Avantia. If the four Beasts of Avantia can find their Chosen Riders they might have the strength to challenge Derthsin. But if they fail, the land of Avantia will be lost forever...

FIRST HERO, CHASING EVIL, CALL TO WAR, FIRE AND FURY OUT NOW!

www.chroniclesofavantia.com